Mrs. McDonald

had a Little Farm

Written by RaeAnn McDonald
Illustrated by Amy McGuire

Mrs. McDonald had a little farm,
E-I-E-I-O

And on that farm she had a horse,
E-I-E-I-O

With a neigh neigh here,
and a neigh neigh there,
here a neigh, there a neigh,
everywhere a neigh neigh!

What? What do you hear?
Neigh Neigh?
That is NOT what I hear!
I hear...

It's about time you
got here!
I'm ready to eat!

Can you scratch my neck?
I've got an itch.

Swat that fly!

Let's go for a ride!

That's what I hear!

Mrs. McDonald had a little farm,
E-I-E-I-O

And on that farm she had two cats,
E-I-E-I-O

With a meow meow here,
and a meow meow there,
here a meow, there a meow,
everywhere a meow meow!

What? What do you hear?
Meow Meow?
That's NOT what I hear!
I hear...

This is my spot.
They're ALL my spots!
I'll sit here!

Fill my dish.
Please feed me.

Leave me alone.

Gotcha!

A mouse!
Play with me!

That's what I
hear!

Mrs. McDonald had a little farm,
E-I-E-I-O

And on that farm she had three dogs,
E-I-E-I-O

With a woof woof here,
and a woof woof there,
here a woof, there a woof,
everywhere a woof woof!

What? What do you hear?
Woof Woof?
That is NOT what I hear!
I hear...

I love you!
Throw it! Throw it!

Rub my belly...
Rub my belly.

You can't get it!
Please try and get it!
Then you can throw it
and I'll get it!

SQUIRREL!

I love you!

That's what I
hear!

Mrs. McDonald had a little farm,
E-I-E-I-O

And on that farm she had some goats,
E-I-E-I-O

With a maaa maaa here,
and a maaa maaa there,
here a maaa, there a maaa,
everywhere a maaa maaa!

What? What do you hear?
Maaa Maaa?
That is NOT what I hear!
I hear...

I can open any gate,
I'll find a way!

I'm king of the
hill!

Where's the feed?
It's in that can!

You can't catch
me!
Watch me run!

That's what I
hear!

Mrs. McDonald had a little farm,
E-I-E-I-O

And on that farm she had some hens,
E-I-E-I-O

With a bawk bawk here,
and a bawk bawk there,
here a bawk, there a bawk,
everywhere a bawk bawk!

What? What do you hear?
Bawk Bawk?
That is NOT what I hear!
I hear...

I just laid an egg!
Oh, I'm the best!

Get the goats out,
we'll clean up...

Let's find some
worms!

That's what I
hear!

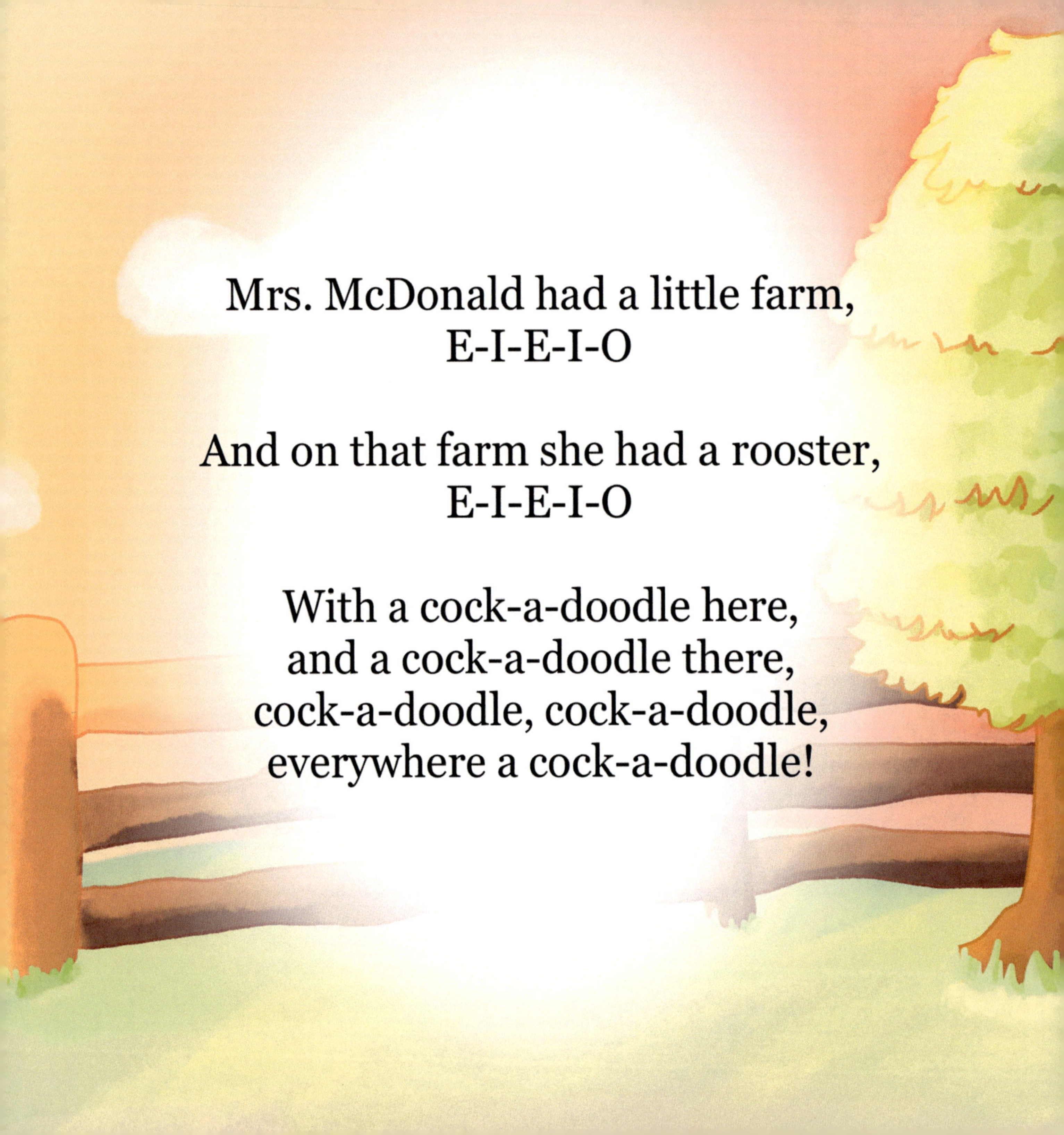

Mrs. McDonald had a little farm,
E-I-E-I-O

And on that farm she had a rooster,
E-I-E-I-O

With a cock-a-doodle here,
and a cock-a-doodle there,
cock-a-doodle, cock-a-doodle,
everywhere a cock-a-doodle!

What? What do you hear?
Cock-a-doodle?
That is NOT what I hear!
I hear...
Wake up!
It's morning!
I'm in charge.

Don't mess with
my hens!

Time to roost,
Let's get to bed.

I'm not afraid of
you!

That's what I
hear!

Mrs. McDonald had a farm,
E-I-E-I-O
And on that farm she had some friends,
E-I-E-I-O

And a meow meow here, and a meow meow there,

With a neigh neigh here, and a neigh neigh there,

And a bawk bawk here, and a bawk bawk there,

And a maaa maaa here, and a maaa maaa there,

And a woof woof
here, and a woof
woof there,

And a cock-a-doodle
here, and a cock-a-
doodle there.

Cock-a-doodle do!

meow!

maaa!
maaa!

bawk!
bawk!

bawk!

Cock-a-doodle!
neigh!
neigh!
Meow!
Meow!
maaa!
maaa!
bawk!
bawk!

Who’s making all this noise?

goodnight!
goodnight!
goodnight!

Goodnight!

Mrs. McDonald had a little farm,
E-I-E-I-O

Made in the USA
Middletown, DE
05 March 2023

26175539R00020